AF424406

The
Return
To
Ai

The fourth book in the series of
The Jeriel Road:
Journey to the land of the Amad.

Dedicated to those who have taught the word in some shape or manner and lived their life by the word in hope of the expected vision that awaits us.

The Return to Ai

Index

The Return to Ai

Prologue:

It is the year 2200 on the planet Arza in the land of Ebal. The city of Ai is still the only known city left and outwardly is the same as when Corbin, Areli, Jamin, Boa and the rescue team left. (The Jeriel Road, Part one)

But not so. On the senuah when the wall door shut an agag was set inside Beth-Pelet to flush out anyone who might be hiding. Within three senuahs Rosh Ibleam fell to an unknown sickness and Zoheleth turned to an unknown teacher of the bahurims when he said he had a solution.

The houses stayed as they were, running them as usual. But Ahithophel convinced Zoheleth to use his new machine to replace Ibleam's form of control. The Deuel stopped when Zoheleth accepted Ahithophel's plan. So comes the beginning of the end.

Phase 1 Discovery: Jada

James 8:32 (KJV) You shall know the truth and the truth shall set you free.

Hidden in the shadows of the fallen pillars of the old temple; blonde haired, blue eyed, seventeen cycles, Elizabeth stood staring at the activities of the various members of the city. She found herself thinking about the old Deuel and realized she was missing the old way that the city would all repeat it together.

Her eyes were drawn by an unusual movement in the bahurim house as some young ones tried escaping their designated rondure. Their cries filled the air but no one listened.

She'd lived here alone for at least seven cycles now and felt quite natural, though at first it felt very strange. Her eyes went back to the bahurims still crying and shook her head in wonder.

She had lived in the alamoth house till one zereda they locked the door with her outside. She wasn't even missed let alone looked for. It was rather difficult getting used to. Food wasn't a problem, the others were used to her working in the guni, so she continued there. It was at cush that she had the problem. She settled on this place cause no one else was allowed to come here.

For a while she was content to be out at all parts of the senuah until one head of the house saw her and she had to sneak away. After that she stayed hidden while it remained light. That worked until some one else saw her.

Once a bahurim noticed her watching. On his

first attempt to get to her he was knocked out when he tried. His efforts changed and he tried something different. He would gradually sidle over toward the fallen pillars pushing the boundaries until she had pity and came to meet him.

Joshua didn't feel he could stay so he left with in a very short span. The next time he came he told her they couldn't get far away from the 'beast' which had some sort of hold on them and 'beast' was an appropriate name for the thing that ran Ai. It had no feelings just order.

Evidently the 'beast' had no way of controlling her. While she didn't know exactly how it happened, she was glad. Joshua called her clear-sighted and she knew what he meant. Clear-sighted shebnis could look into another shebni's eyes where as all others had to face off to the side, they couldn't stand the full gaze of the clear-sighted.

Elizabeth switched her attention to a well known athurim hanging near several bahurims who were standing around talking. That standing around talking was another change. Joshua had said no one was allowed talking much even yet though they were allowed when not assigned any job or in a class. Few classes existed any more, that had been Zoheleth's idea and he was gone. Some hung on for the routine's sake. That also included the practice of being an athurim who liked to tell on others. This athurim was one of the few left and must be very good or he wouldn't still be around.

She felt a breeze and a single word brought her head around and her mind back to the old Deuel. 'Pekahiah!' It rekindled her previous thoughts. What was that? The Deuel? How did it go? 'Pekahiah... Ahasbai... Betah... Addi... Jeshanah?'

Shaking her head in disgust Elizabeth flipped the length of her hair back over her shoulders where it hung almost to her waist, uncut since she'd left and come here. She sighed. The pattern of the words were gone, she could no longer remember the order. Sadly enough for she had a feeling they had been important. Well she could be thankful she had her freedom.

So how had she escaped the 'beast'? That question puzzled Elizabeth, running over and over in her mind. She could remember the Adinos coming to the house. It happened that she had been sent to the guni for fresh carpas. Instinctively she had hid when they came and went taking a lot of the alamoths with them. Her instinct made her stay in the guni till they returned and she quickly rejoined the group when laying down. From that point on she made herself act like the rest. That must have been when it happened. How glad she was she could escape to these ruins.

From the temple chemosh, she watched the city working. It gave her a strange feeling about what was in the wind. She could almost smell it.

This shahar, she worked in the younger guni and smuggled her stash back. Her plans were to work in the Migdol's guni later as Sisamai went to the apad.

Her eyes noticed the bahurim sidling towards her boundaries. Joshua must have some news, he thought she would want. He was getting older and felt he should be listened to. Even now he saw where she sat and ventured to try to reach her. She climbed down coming beneath the fallen pillars a new limit. He was getting braver in his ventures.

"Hello, Joshua."

He eyed her, "You aren't to be in here you know." She studied him observing how his eyes shied away from her direct gaze.

"If I can't be here, how come I'm not hurting?"

That made him stop and think. Joshua wasn't sure how to answer. A yell from his rondure sent him away and Elizabeth drifted back through her path among the pillars. She needed more food but it would have to wait.

Setting back on top of the chemosh where the pillars were the thickest, she chewed on carpas. Once dried they were very tough but provided enough food to stop the belly from hurting. She spied Joshua making his way back. Waiting to see if he would make it, she hopped down retracing her steps.

Joshua greeted her again. "You are free!

That's why you can be here. I can feel it.

Elizabeth once again studied his young face. "Are you going to tell?"

Joshua shook his head slowly, "No, I want to be free too. If I turn you in, I'll never learn how. Do you know?"

"No I don't but I will try to learn. You'll have to return shortly. Where do you hurt when it starts?"

Joshua touched his shoulder reaching behind his neck. "Here." he started to say and went down. Elizabeth checked his unconscious body. He'd lost thought but seemed none the worse so she waited. Mean while she studied the back of his neck while feeling the back of her own.

When he came to himself, she told him, "You have something in your neck. I don't but I don't know how to get it out. Go back to your guni and I will think about it. Oh and see if any others want this too."

Without another word, Joshua headed back. He knew of a few bahurims that he'd been talking with who were interested. He only hoped she could help.

Elizabeth's interest now became more personal. Not only did she watch the shebnis, she kept a better look on the bahurims. At one point she counted eight bahurims hanging around Joshua. They took extra care not to exceed their allotted time for talking.

Occasionally that deuel word popped back in her mind. Just out of no where, "Pekahiah."

Elizabeth didn't pay it any mind. True it was the beginning of the Deuel, but what did that have to do with what she wanted?

Several senuahs passed in the usual until one shahar Elizabeth woke hearing something different. Feet walking, the sound echoed through the ground. Quickly rising to her perch she saw the assir door open. Out filed a row of shebnis, carrying very large rocks with holes cut in the center. Coming from the bahurim side of Castle Migdol, it took two shebnis to carry each rock and even then they strained in the effort since the holes would fit themselves.

Ahithophel brought up the end, talking and gesturing with his hands. The words weren't clear but the hand motions sent them through the gates. In a short while he returned with a second line of shebnis leading them out the assir's door. He motioned for them to climb the walls and mount the top, stopping at certain postings.

Elizabeth watched amazed. Still hungry she dropped from her perch, grabbed more dried carpas and returned to watch . If the shebni wasn't in the exact spot Ahithophel had marked, he would jump, yell and point before climbing up and illustrating what was needed. Climbing back down, he would disappear outside the gates, be there briefly and return for more yelling.

At last he returned leading those from outside back inside the castle. In a few moments they returned carrying more blocks. They were placed where they had been standing. The shebnis were sent inside again for another load. These were slightly shaped different and placed on the ground inside the wall directly beneath the shebnis perched on top of the city's encircling rock wall. When a rock was placed on the ground, the shebni on top came down; picked up the rock and carried it to the top. This work took the entire senuah closing out with cush's darkness.

When all activity stopped seemingly silent for cush, Elizabeth could stand it no longer. Leaving her refuge, she slipped over and through the gates which had been left open.

What she saw only confused her more. The rocks encircled all the city except the temple portion. A pile placed outside matched the ones inside. Perhaps exactly the same position. The lead rock lay on its side leaving a certain amount of distance between it and the wall. The next had the hollowed part a minute higher that the first, making the holes match with the second slightly elevated.

Feeling uneasy being out in the open, Elizabeth hurried back inside slipping up to her perch where she climbed under. Curling up in her arpad, she slept.

Early shahar, the noise picked back up as the

shebnis and Ahithophel resumed their work. The
increase in activity made Elizabeth think it might be
better not to continue working in the guni. So she
decided to do more exploring in the temple's
underground rooms.

She had already discovered two additional
rooms which connected with what she was using.
This time she decided to investigate the second
small room. She was pleasantly surprised to find
another smaller room which wasn't in too bad of
shape. There were other dark rooms which were
badly damaged. She couldn't be certain they were
safe. A number of chunks of rocks had doorways
blocked.

Sniffing the air around the fallen walls, she
shook her head returning to the open air. That air
really stunk. On the chemosh perch, the fresh air
made her remember the last senuah the chemosh had
been used. The burnt wood was so ugly. Shivering,
she suppressed that memory, replacing it with
another one less horrible. Ahithophel had taken over
and the leaders in each house grew lazy so they were
the first to visit the beast.

The next step was easy, for the head of each
house passively sent the shebnis in rows. That was
when the adinos came. That had to be when the
implants were successfully place at the hairlines at
the back of the necks like Joshua. Since the leaders
first accepted what ever was said, they didn't look

any further. But what about the ones who didn't want something in the back of their necks? Like herself.

Elizabeth returned to the smallest room. If she was to help like she felt, she needed more space than what she had now. Not only for bodies, but also for food.

In one corner of the room a small roof section had cracked letting in some light. Choosing another corner she built an agag, very small, and hung zibas and carpas close to it. As the food dried, she went to the next room picking a wall to hang containers of storage. Lining the floor she used her meager supply of chargers and bakbuks. She'd replace them during cush. The dark hid her well.

Some of her previous training included asa-that of healing the body when sick. This training was before the beast for now it took care of all that. But the asa training had taught her possible solutions for taking care of aches and pains. Parts of the zibas would work to form the mixtures.

Ideas came while sleeping. When awake she put the ideas into practice. She kept watch and had counted close to ten rocks in each of the outer stacks outside the wall. Each of the rocks connected to the previous one.

Joshua had been given a new addition to his chores,. He was now the shebni responsible for delivering zibas and carpas to the castle. She knew each house contributed the same amount.

Joshua's work also gave him responsibility of some of the smaller bahurims; teaching how to be obedient and do their assigned work so not to receive colosse. Several senuahs passed before Elizabeth saw Joshua begin making small variations in his usual routine. Sometimes, he'd touch the arm of another bahurim in passing. When he first did it, she dismissed the incident as nothing. Not until later did she see the bahurims were always the same ones. In some of her food runs she saw him gradually add more. It all appeared so innocent no one appeared to notice.

Late one zereda while lying in the room directly beneath the chemosh, she stared around mentally going over available space. What could be done? Should be done? Quite a few could fit here or even in the next room. Possibly even in her newest discovery. It was empty. When the temple fell it didn't hurt any inner rooms underneath it. When it collapsed only the outside fell.

But even if they hid here, the beast would torture them for being out of place and send the adinos to take them back.

As she drifted off to sleep an idea began forming. Early shahar she rose and watched as each house woke. When the first one went to the guni, she went also cleaning the outer edges, filling her salma before slipping back to where she slept.

Frugal in her task she took care not to overload all at once for she knew how they kept tally.

Mid senuah found her mingling with the older shebnis from the alamoth side of the castle. Again she filled her salmas and slipped off when done.

Keeping an eye on the head, she watched as the alamoths finished heading back inside their house and the door shut. She knew not to return. Storing her haul she took various pieces to the smaller room hanging them close to the small agag. She rebuilt it when the fire dwindled. These would dry and could be reheated in water and eaten.

Phase 2: Shear-Jashub: Commissioned

Luke 4:18; The spirit of the Lord is on me because he has anointed me, to preach good news to the poor. He has sent me to proclaim freedom for the prisoners and recovery of sight for the blind, to release the oppressed...

Raguel and Shamah strolled slowly through Benaiah's guni. Actually it belonged to them all. No one had to worry about food here, it was plentiful and anyone could eat at any time.

The new carpas and zibas tasted exceptionally good. The only thing Raguel had difficulty in adjusting to: no one served anyone else except Benaiah. It was easy to serve him. Jedidah stayed near him constantly and it wasn't any wonder she blossomed under his love and kindness.

Their bodies were different though. For they could think of a place and be there. Benaiah chuckled the first time it happened to Shamah. She'd been out walking and thought of him. Instantly she was standing before him basking in his warm love. But the surprise on her face finding herself there delighted Benaiah and he laughed.

His chuckle brought a quick grin in response and she tried a repeat thought of the guni. Her departure caught Jedidah unprepared for she was coming up the steps carrying a charger. Shamah heard the clang of it falling as she went. She laughed too.

There were more to learn about this new land. They could jump higher and land easier. They learned games to play with the younger. Yet in spite of all the fun, both Raguel and Shamah were having a difficult time in settling in.

It never got dark, so no cush. They very

seldom tired. No one telling them what to do and no arguments. Salmas never got dirty and neither did they. Every so often all were required to gather in Benaiah's presence for a sharing meal and he would take time to talk with each one. Some who liked it would sing. Others would dance and bow before him.

Benaiah had warned of a transition process but instead of getting settled, Raguel could feel himself getting more restless and beginning to think about returning to the city. Not wanting to appear ungracious, he said nothing hoping it would pass.

Once when strolling together later, Shamah was staring around. This place had held all her hopes and dreams. Yet now she was here, it wasn't enough. There was something missing as if undone.

She thought back to the road they'd traveled. It had been long and hard. Several cycles had passed. Yet she didn't feel all that much older. Deep inside an inexplicable urge was rising to be on the move again.

On that thought she blinked and came to a stand still. When you got here where did you move on to? A quick glance at Raguel brought a knowing, he felt the same.

What should they do? Why should they feel this way? The rest certainly seemed happy enough. Why were they so different?

"Shamah, come!" Benaiah's voice sounded so

good in her mind's eye. The rush of love swept over her making her eager to obey.

"Raguel, Benaiah wants me." She informed him eager to be gone. Raguel was still just learning to hear. Then Shamah quickly shut her ears down as Benaiah's voice boomed through mind and space.

"Raguel, I need you too."

"I'm to come as well." Raguel happily informed Shamah, though he knew she had already heard.

Her transition was smoother than his but they arrived at the same instant. Jedidah greeted them warmly then returned to Benaiah's side. He shared a smile with her before facing the other two.

"What's going on?" His question caught Raguel off guard but Shamah was ready.

"Benaiah, I'm feeling unsettled. I mean I've tried to be satisfied but I have a sense that my road is not finished. As if I've left a job undone. I don't want to appear ungrateful but I don't feel right in staying. Is it possible to go back?" Then she remembered Corbin and her face brightened.

Raguel's head swiveled at her first words, surprised to hear his thoughts expressed; Benaiah began smiling, his face glowing with satisfaction.

"Of course. This is good. I was hoping you would notice. Your answer is yes,. I have need of some help back in Ai for there is unfinished business. The planet Arza must be destroyed. But before I do, others who want to come must have someone to lead them. It won't be your same road, for the place you left no longer exists as you knew it. I have one alamoth," he bowed toward Shamah making her smile, "who hears the old Deuel slightly. The time you both knew is over and they aren't allowed to speak it. It is forgotten... almost."

He smiled lovingly, "I did say almost. Several are free and do hear my voice. They listen as much as they know how. The one I will be sending you to," he nodded to Shamah, " is called Elizabeth. And yours Raguel is called Azmah." Their faces began to glow as his meaning became clear. "Yes this desire is from me. I am glad that you are willing."

Nervously Jedidah moved closer and he sent her a reassuring smile. "No, my dear, you are not to go. You want to stay and here you will be.

Raguel, during your time of waiting, practice listening by opening your thoughts. Letting others in will help you hear. For you must learn to hear without me being so loud.

Shamah, you must be willing to listen for other's thoughts. Now I know," Benaiah held up his hand upon her gesture of distaste. "You do not like to intrude. But hearing their thoughts will keep you in tune with my leading. I give you permission to listen. So," he waved his hand briskly, "I release you to continue your lessons. You do not leave yet, the plans at the city are not presently in place. When they are, you will know and be ready."

His radiant smile warmed Shamah and she nodded. Holding thought in mind, she gave one wave and vanished. Basking in the warmth his smile generated Raguel found himself almost envying Jedidah. A tug at his mind reminded him, he was also loved and had no reason to feel that way. Giving an off center grin, he also vanished, emerging close to Shamah. A deep thanksgiving settled in. They were going back.

Phase 3; Agur: gathering, assembler

Proverbs 30:4 (KJV) Who has ascended up into heaven, or descended? Who has gathered the wind in his fists? Who has bound the waters in a garment? Who has established all the ends of the earth? What is his name and what is his son's name; if you can tell?

Elizabeth's search continued. Exactly what she was searching for, she wasn't sure but as she climbed over fallen rocks and debris, she knew she was about to find it. The first thing she noticed was the air which had been a strong odor now was beginning to freshen. And in that last room which showed less rubble, some of the walls and door frames were still standing. Parts of the walls held up faded old tapestries.

Elizabeth wiped a dusty hand through her hair smudging her forehead while attempting to crawl over another particularly large wall block. A soft breeze caressed her cheek. Immediately her curiosity stirred. Another opening? She realized the air smelled much fresher at this point, not as dusty. On the other side once over the block, a door still stood shut.

Elizabeth opened it stepping into what appeared to have been a hall at one time. In fact it seemed to be a continuation of the previous hall which was blocked. Now it extended only as far as the next room before being blocked again by fallen blocks. But this next room was in real good shape, not very dirty but also no other door. It appeared to be the end of her search.

No! Not possible, the air was too fresh. She stepped back a ways studying the entire room. The tapestry bugged her, pulling her to it. Print long faded seemingly not able to be seen yet it moved.

How? What was the secret? She touched it, brushing against the picture. It gave. Reaching forward she grabbed the bottom corner, looking inside. Darkness hid what was there so she stuck her other hand stepping inside, feeling around.

Another tapestry hung there. Eagerly she pushed it back revealing another room with a door. Opening the door revealed a similar hall with huge rocks lying to the left but clear floor led to the right. She was past the blockage. Down the hall another door yielded another room entrance. The fallen rocks stopped any forward passage without entering the room.

Inside the room, another tapestry hung where by she entered yet another room. It was then she realized the light had darkened and she was hungry. Denying her desire to continue, she retraced her path stepping out in her sleeping room.

Her drinking and bathing water came from an ain in the center. It was another reason she'd chosen the place for sleeping. Cush was settling over the city so grabbing some food she climbed onto her perch scanning the view.

All seemed pretty quiet so after eating Elizabeth slipped down and cut out through the fallen pillars gathering more carpas and zibas. Upon her return she stayed long enough to put everything in its place then back she went to investigate the outside city walls.

What the...? Elizabeth stared at the assembly in progress. Blocks had been added to the prior ones lined up with the ones topping the walls. The hollowed out squares fit snugly as if making a passage or tunnel though the air. When completed of course. Now they were roughly a third up and a third down. The walls no longer crumbled. They had been repaired and felt smooth to the touch.

In taktuk's dim light Elizabeth could see the wall had been braced. Realizing she'd been studying the partial construction long enough, she quietly retraced her steps, still puzzled over what she'd seen. Something big was happening. Why else would they be doing this? And what was this? What was it for? Maybe Joshua would know.

Early shahar, Elizabeth woke with a sense of danger. She sat up knowing the change was only beginning. 'Pekahiah.'

*   *   *

She was leaving at the darkness. The coming darkness. This coming darkness. Her shem named her survivor though she was unaware of it. Sarid only knew her time was coming and soon that which was growing within her body would be expelled and taken.

She wanted to keep it. Eglah or ahilud she didn't care. And if she stayed they would take it a

way where she wouldn't know. So the time to go
was this senuah when sisamai fell.

But go where? Where could she go for safety?
How would they live? She was going no matter
what, Sarid thought purposing to go deep into the
lower levels of the castle. It wasn't out of her
assigned area so the beast wouldn't sound the alarm.
The only problem she could have would be the
delivery. With no one to help it could be rough.

Still her naama would not have the pain giver.
Sarid didn't care if she ceased to exist, she would
pay the price for her naama to be free.

Heavily Sarid got off her arpad to carry out her
duties. Not doing her duties would cause attention
she didn't want. Everything must be as usual. There
must be no cause for alarm.

*   *   *

Ahithophel paused in his perusal of the beast's
readouts. What did these little checks mean?
Something strange was in the works. Some
bahurims were changing their routines. Not enough
to bring colosse. Their actions were all within the
acceptable limits. His thoughts caused him to miss
the little check pattern beside Sarid's shem
signifying her coming birth. All prospective births
were monitored for it accomplished two thing: a
record and the implanting. As he scanned the list

again Ahithophel's mind went to the construction on the walls of Ai.

Abaddon had alerted him to the coming danger when everyone would have to leave Ai. Where it sat was in the center of the area, the beast called: Hon-Hegidgad-Hill of thunder.

The beast was truly a marvel. Not only did it keep everyone in line; keep track of births; it also recorded every movement of Arza.

Ahithophel's knowledge of asa -cures for the pains of the body enabled him to place the tiny mechanical insert where it would do the most good. He'd been the one Ibleam had accidentally allowed to see the process used to remove ahava-the essence of the shebnis life force. Yet somehow Ahithophel realized the process was not the answer. Secretly he set up his own zarephath in the lower levels of the temple. His studies produced a new invention-the beast.

All his leaders liked it at first. Fights among the younger bahurims quickly dropped and orders were accepted easier.

More acceptable changes were seen later after the take over. It had taken him about ten cycles before he got up enough nerve to approach the ruthless Abaddon who quickly recognized its possibilities and together they planned the take-over of Ai.

Their plan fell quickly into place when

Zoheleth and Ibleam ceased to exist. While their bodies burnt in the chemosh, Abaddon stepped up to take leadership.

Later when the temple pillars began to crack and fall, shock of their breaking made it simple for his rule to be established and his appointing Ahithophel to fill Ibleam's office. Ahithophel quickly brought the inserts into the mix calming the overwhelming fear that was causing problems. Of course neither he nor Abaddon had any. Their rule brought many changes by deteriorating spirits in the houses as the alamoths and bahurims were then used for Abaddon's own advantages.

*   *   *

Azmah walked steadily in the food prep room of castle Migdol. Hands were constantly active though his eyes saw everyone he passed. He missed nothing and was quick to spot Sarid's drooping shoulders signifying her tiredness.

He saw the expression in her eyes in several brief glimpses and knew something was different. There appeared to be a singular purpose in them and he resolved to keep an eye on her. It was her time to deliver.

*   *   *

Elizabeth was back up at shahar. She resumed her exploration of the passage. Deeper and deeper she ventured into the darkness following the faintest glimmer of light in the shadows ahead. The light brew brighter as the passage seemed to rise. Several small wind-holes revealed the source of the fresh air. They gave greater vision and she gazed at those in open mouth wonder. This was part of the castle. The part she could see from her perch.

Suddenly the passage was cut off by a huge tapestry similar to those she'd seen below. Elizabeth came to a halt poised to flee should anything sound abnormal. She could hear vague sounds of activity and withdrew a few steps in retreat. Judging by the dust on the floor, this wasn't being used but those voices were alarming in their volume.

In fact from where she stood Elizabeth could hear a strange whine that seemed to vibrate up through her feet and ankles. It puzzled her having not been inside the castle before and forgetting her fear she retreated along the passage trying to trace its start.

The noise grew the loudest at a relatively new doorway. Not being too deeply embedded below the wind holes light, Elizabeth could see the lack of use here too in spite of being newer that the rest. Tentatively she put her hand out touching the door. It swung open easily.

*   *   *

Azmah was heading for after mid-meal training classes, having finished his assigned chores, when he caught sight of a strange door opening and a figure framed in an entrance he had not noticed ever. The glimpse spurred him into immediate action as the door shut and he leaped intercepting its closing. He managed to get his hand hooked around the edge, reopening and sliding through, pulling it shut behind. He followed the figure.

Elizabeth's heart was pounding. What had she done? The unthinkable had happened. Why did that shebni have to be there when the door opened? And how could he follow her? Why had he even noticed? Usually if someone did they assumed she was on assignment like them.

Not used to running she began loosing ground. Desperation set in as his steps closed. Making a wrong turn brought her up against a pile of fallen rocks. Resolutely she turned to face what was to come.

Azmah could hear her gasping breath then her footsteps stop. He slowed his accordingly before rounding the corner coming face to face. Amazingly her eyes showed no fear only resolution. She faced him head on, not looking to the side. Curiosity reigned.

Taking in her dusty appearance which was beautiful, he had a thought her salma didn't do her justice. Something within made him want to know who she was.

His words popped out, "Who are you?" They

brought wonder to her eyes. Wonder at his smooth deep tone of voice and the fact he asked instead of demanded. Her eyes examined him in turn coming back to study his face. Kindness she responded to and something else, she wasn't sure what but it gave a feeling that he could be trusted. She decided.

"I'm Elizabeth of the temple. Who are you?" Her query brought a response accompanied with a slight smile accompanied by a twinkle in his eye.

"I'm Azmah of the castle. The temple?"

"Yes, I live free." Her choice of words shocked him and her both. His next words drew her out more.

"I am free also." Puzzlement kept her studying him.

"But you are of the castle?"

"Yes, but I am free. Where are you staying?"

"I'm of the temple."

Disbelief flared. "It's in ruins. How can you be there? Abaddon did away with the chemarims."

"I know. I'm not a chemarim and only the top is in ruins. I stay below."

He gestured, "How did you get here?"

"This passage goes to the temple ruins."

Her answer made him pause in thought. "All the way?"

"Yes!"

"I must think on this. I also must leave or I will be missed. Will you come back later after zereda?"

She moved consciously, "I might."

Amusement flickered, "I might need your help."

She nodded watching as he walked a way retracing his steps. Moments later she emerged in the ruins of the temple resuming her perch. She waited.

*   *   *

Sarid could sense the contraction building but had no time to prepare. Indeed she'd never experienced anything like this before. The second pain bent her double and she faked acting as though she had dropped something. Biting hard on her lip to hide the pain, she was relieved when the next one was slower and not as hard. She managed to straighten resuming zereda meal preparations. Her eyes circled the room coming in contact with one other pair of eyes. She broke the contact quickly fearful of what he might see.

Her next contraction was lighter yet and she breathed easier. She could handle those. Dropping her tools in the wash caphtor, she exited the food area unsure now where to go. If she went too far, the beast would sound the warning but any excessive rise in temperature would do it also.

Foot steps coming from behind sent her

reeling with fear. *'Think Sarid, think.'*

A soft husky voice spoke, "Come, I know of a place where you can hide."

She jumped when he spoke almost taking off in a run. His words stopped her. "Hide?"

"Yes,"

Her nod came on the wave of another contraction. She choked the scream in her throat. "Hurry!"

A strong arm took hers and propelled her forward.

*   *   *

Elizabeth waited breathlessly hidden within viewing distance of the door. When it opened she stood. Seeing the two shebnis, she held back.

"Elizabeth?"

The whisper coupled with a muffled scream brought her forward. Azmah's eyes greeted her while his words caught her unprepared.

"The naama comes."

"Is she free?"

"No."

"Then they know."

"Maybe. Maybe she slipped by. Sometimes they do."

"Then not all are bound."

"No. But take care of her. The young one is

Habaiah."

"Habaiah?"

"Yes," he helped them move down the passage a ways then Sarid stopped.

"This is my limit. The beast will know."

"I must return." Azmah helped her lie down before withdrawing. Elizabeth knelt beside her.

Sarid looked up. "Do you know what to do?"

"Yes."

"Don't let them take it to the beast. I want it free."

"I won't." Elizabeth's words were cut off by the pain and even in the dark Sarid's face went white.

Wishing she'd brought her own asa supplies Elizabeth waited thinking. The supplies would at least helped with the pain. She held Sarid's hands letting her grip tightly then removing her own outer salma she placed it beneath Sarid.

The pain came quicker. She checked on the naama as Sarid gave one more shudder and collapsed. Tenderly Elizabeth brought the eglah into her arms, the lusty cry testifying of a set of healthy lungs. It was then she heard the steps and turned to look.

It was Azmah and one look told her the bad news; they knew. He leaned over lifting Sarid and Elizabeth quickly cut the cord and they set out, herself taking the lead.

No words were necessary. The rapid steps weren't far behind. Elizabeth held the naama close and she stopped crying.

Occasionally Sarid's body would twitch and flail revealing the pain being inflicted by the beast. When they reached the first of the debris, Elizabeth led Azmah into the second room behind the tapestry.

He laid Sarid down resting his arms. Using hand motions Elizabeth tried to convince him to stay. He stared at her for an instant then nodded. Elizabeth took the naama with her.

Beneath the chemosh, she washed and wrapped the naama snugly. Then grabbing asaph and asa supplies she headed back.

Sounds of departing steps proceeded her arrival and the sight of Sarid on the floor brought a fresh anger. Her body was tilted and twisted as if in a frantic struggle. One she hadn't won. Even as Elizabeth watched she realized the struggle continued. No one had done this, just the beast.

Sarid took one last breath and sank into repose. Her eyes stared straight ahead. Numbly Elizabeth sank to the floor sensing she was gone.

Suddenly she was infused into doing what she had intended to do. She could inject the asa under the skin. Cradling the naama in her lap, she slid the asa in place. At the point when she shoved the needle she spoke the only word on her mind.

"Pekahiah!"

The other voices speaking with hers made her turn. No one was there. Not even Azmah. Why he left, she didn't know unless it was to draw off attention.

She remembered the departing footsteps. It did sound like more than one set. Maybe he had no choice.

Elizabeth didn't want to move. She was still sitting next to Sarid's still body. Everything was so quiet and peaceful.

Something stirred by her side where Sarid lay. The motion made her jump, bringing her head around. In surprise she watched as Sarid took a weak breath. Then another and another gradually getting stronger. She raised herself up staring at her blood soaked salmas.

Elizabeth said what was in her head. "The naama is here. Do not be alarmed."

Sarid's dazed expression didn't change. "What?"

"She's here. She's alright. What is her shem?'

"I-I-I'm not sure. What do you suggest?"

"Well Azmah said she was Habaiah."

"Habaiah?"

Elizabeth nodded. She could understand Sarid's confusion.

"Yes, I like that." Sarid laid back down.

"We must leave. When you are able." Elizabeth rose to her feet.

"My head feels funny, strange. Very, very odd. I don't know if I can stand. How did I get here?"

"Azmah carried you. The beast had sounded the alert and the Adinos were sent."

Sarid tentatively swiveled her neck. "There's no pain. I can't feel anything."

"Let me look." Elizabeth waited for Sarid to pull back her hair before placing her own hand up to feel.

Her exclamation jerked Sarid upright.

"It's out. The beast must have kicked it out. Apparently when you ceased breathing, it decided you no longer mattered."

Wonder and amazement filled Sarid's eyes though darkening shadows hindered Elizabeth from seeing. "How am I breathing then?"

"I trained some as an asa, and have supplies. Yet when you gave your last breath I thought you were gone. Then something or someone urged me to give you the medicine any way and speak one word."

"What word?"

"Pekahiah!"

"I remember that word. Part of the old deuel. And that brought me back?"

"It must have. It was the strangest thing: when I said it, it sounded like lots of voices speaking. As if more than just me. Can you stand?"

"I think so now, though I may be a little

wobbly."

Her first shaky steps confirmed it. "Can I lean on you? I don't seem to be able to judge space very well."

Elizabeth placed Sarid's hand on her shoulder while holding Habaiah close. Very, very slowly the three headed for the temple.

Phase 4: Arcturus: more gathering

I King 19:18 (KJV) For I have left me seven thousand in Israel, all the knees which have not bowed unto Baal, and every mouth which has not kissed him.

Azmah reluctantly left the twitching form on the ground covered floor. Part of him wanted to stay but part told him he might get exposed. He had to resume his duties or someone either Baashah or Bera would be checking on him. They were always trying to catch someone in the act of being in the wrong place. He didn't want to reveal his freedom and he didn't want the insert either.

The other steps he had been hearing suddenly paused then retreated and he understood. Sarid lived no longer. At least the naama lived. Elizabeth would take care of it, somehow. She'd lived this long outside of the houses. How glad he was, she did.

*   *   *

Elizabeth had a quandary. Habaiah seemed to always need feeding and Sarid had little food to give. This was one area Elizabeth wasn't prepared for and didn't know how to handle. The answer came unexpectedly from Sarid.

Being released from the beast caused Sarid to have to relearn everything. For it had controlled her entire system even to foot pressure and weight sensors in her mind. The nerve endings had restructured and she felt really good. It was simply learning how to balance that required such patience.

Seeing Elizabeth's problem she though it over.

Beth-Alamoth seemed the logical place for Habaiah since they had the food supply needed. But how to get her in without raising suspicions. Her suggestion brought relief to Elizabeth.

"No problem! I'll ask Azmah. He said there were others who were free as well. I'll check at mid-meal." Elizabeth hadn't been back since the birth and she suddenly felt anxious to see him.

Moments later she headed for the passage, packing Habaiah, who for once was quiet. The walking kept her asleep, packed securely against Elizabeth's chest.

She was gratified to find little disturbance at the first exit and very careful not to open the door as she had before.

He wasn't there at the moment and it didn't look as if he had been. She sat to wait until the zereda meal. Her short wait was rewarded by the door opening and Azmah stepping in. Breathlessly she waited making sure he was alone.

*   *   *

Azmah couldn't get Elizabeth off his mind. Wishing to see her brought him to the entrance twice a senuah to check. He'd about given up this senuah for when he stepped through, no clues gave her away. He turned to exit and heard a rustle as she rose emerging from the corner.

"Elizabeth!"

"Yes." They approached each other.

"Are you alright?" Both queries came simultaneously, bringing assurances for both sides. Elizabeth picked up the conversation.

"I do need some help. Little Habaiah needs more to eat than Sarid has to give. Is there a way you can slip her into Beth-Alamoth without anyone knowing?"

Azmah picked up on Sarid's shem. "Then she still exists? How can that be when the beast thinks she has ceased? What happened?"

"You are correct that the beast thinks she has ceased. I gave her a shot of asa spoke Pekahiah and she started moving. Just as if she woke."

"Wow, just like that! Pekahiah! Well I never." Azmah marveled then remembered, "Any way, to get to your problem, the answer is yes. Another naama has been born and they are inserting the chip now. We couldn't get to her in time. Besides the shebni wasn't concerned. So what was her shem you said?"

"Well you told me she was Habaiah so I took your advice."

"How wonderful. When can you bring her?"

"I have her now." Elizabeth untied Habaiah laying her in his arms. Azmah tenderly held her head before studying Elizabeth. His warm eyes made her feel good though vaguely uneasy. Picking up her feelings he spoke, "I'd better go. Is there any way I can let you know when you are needed?"

Elizabeth thought it over. "No, I'll just come over each senuah about this same time. Will that do?"

Azmah wanted to say no, but he held his tongue. He hid his excitement about being able to see her. "That is wonderful. Now I have to go.!" He looked at her again before stepping through the door.

Elizabeth retraced her steps to Sarid, passing on the good news. She found her sitting on Elizabeth's perch in the old chemosh. Surprisingly enough, Sarid was beginning to walk much better with only three senuahs of relearning.

"He's got her and will slip her in during cush's early darkness. They have another naama to slip her in with."

Sarid kept looking over the city. "I'm glad. I think you'd better take a look up here."

Elizabeth climbed beside her studying the newly constructed wall attachments. They looked finished now but something strange was happening. Each shebni that had been assigned to the top of the wall was now climbing inside the new rocks. Moments later they appeared at the bottom emerging only to climb back up and do it again.

Elizabeth and Sarid stared at each other searching for answers. A movement on the outer edge of the ruins drew Elizabeth's attention and she observed Joshua's direction in his walking.

"Stay here. I'll be back." Elizabeth dropped down from her perch managing to arrive in their meeting place before he did. Something was different with him when he came. "What's up?"

"You're right something's wrong. They are beginning to suspect those who have been coming to talk. It's made me very careful. Here a while back Ahithophel called in and asked questions about the others. Elizabeth, is there a way to be out of the beast's control? I've got to get away."

"Joshua, I have been searching and there is a way. However since they are being suspicious of your actions, is this the best time to do it? Is there anyone you haven't talked with that might want to do it too? Once you take the steps, you know, you can't be seen in the open."

As he listened, her calm words brought reason and peace. And when her words sank in, Joshua began thinking.

"You're right. There are probably more. I can't disappear yet. So what do I do?"

"What you've always done. Above all don't get up tight. Apparently the beast can tell. If you need to tell those who are coming to slack off coming as much, do it."

"Can you tell me anything for the others to go on?"

Elizabeth looked at him long and straight. "Just say Pekahiah, that's your code. And observe those who respect the word. Those who do not-be careful around them."

Joshua's brown eyes drifted as his thinking turned inward considering those who had been coming. "Okay. These last couple of senuahs, has brought a couple of new ones. When they talk, they don't seem real. I guess that is what set me off."

He paused, taking a deep breath, "Thanks, I'm glad you tell me no more than necessary. It makes it easy not to tell anything."

She grinned, "I want to be your fr-ie-nd too. One more thing, if you need to get me word, talk to a tall blonde haired shebni in the castle. His shem is Azmah."

His shocked expression made her eye him questionably. "What's wrong?"

"He's right under Bera in control."

"Yes?"

"You don't understand, he works for them."

"Listen, because of him a little naama is alive and free. And I found the answer for you. Don't go on appearances. If you need help, give him the code and then watch what he does."

"I see. Otherwise I say nothing. Right?"

*   *   *

Ozni hurried carrying Habaiah. His nineteen cycles made it possible for him to remember before the beast did and often heard words from the deuel. Not that he had paid much attention to it until now, since Azmah told him about what had happened to Habaiah's shebni and how she still lived. Pekahiah. He spoke it in his mind and again heard the many voices saying it with him.

His mind was diverted from his train of thought by his entrance to Beth-shan and being greeted by Anna. She took both naamas, eyes revealing no secrets even though his were quizzical. Her departure was only broken when she turned at the door and glanced back.

"Ozni."

"Anna."

He left after she shut the door.

*   *   *

Anna nervously placed each naama in tiny arpads. Habaiah was awake and looking up at her. Anna's heart was touched as she recognized true sight in the gaze of the little one. It was so refreshing to see a naama who could.

As she unwrapped her to change the bottom wrap Anna came across letters on the cloth. They spelled out Habaiah and she nodded. Better remove that so she remained well hidden. She promptly followed up her thoughts taking all evidence before writing in the records of both shems.

*   *   *

Elizabeth and Sarid were proceeding according to Elizabeth's foresight. Her first priority consisted of food storage. Sarid was better at this due to her experience at the castle so Elizabeth put it in her capable hands. Elizabeth kept watch over the city-making raids on the gunis and trips to the castle.

What ever the rock formations were, they were now fully completed. Ahithophel assigned many of the shebnis to patching the inside walls now and clearing any debris left by the previous workers.

Elizabeth met several times with Joshua asking about the huge rocks. He hadn't heard but promised to listen more.

When she met with Azmah, she never thought of asking for he always made her feel strange. Elizabeth helped deliver a couple bahurim naamas but the alamoths chose to stay in the castle. They'd delivered so easily, the beast hadn't any record of the change and due to his preoccupation, Ahithophel didn't catch the births or check the beast's records of the newly arrived with the number of the inserts. For now it went very smooth.

One senuah Azmah joined Elizabeth carrying a sense of excitement. It bubbled under the surface.

When the door closed he blurted out the news taking hold of Elizabeth's shoulders in his excitement.

"They've finished the walls. The beast says we must prepare for danger. It claims an attack is being readied. So we must be ready." His excitement was contagious. Elizabeth finally thought to ask.

"What are those things?"

"Escape tunnels. Everyone is to use them and will be taught how. Once I find out I'll show you."

Without thinking Elizabeth smiled up at Azmah only to discover his face was amazingly close to hers and that strange gaze had come back. It did something to her insides, making them sort of flip flop.

When he noticed her uneasiness, Azmah backed off releasing her arms though continuing talking.

"Some of the bahurims have been speaking to me briefly. One mentioned Pekahiah."

Elizabeth looked startled. "That must be Joshua testing you. I told him you were alright."

Azmah forced himself to turn a way. It was getting harder and harder to leave her. That must not be. Yet the attraction was so great, he could barely deal with it.

"I must go. You will be back again?"

"Yes, If you need me."

Oh, I need you. I need you, Azmah thought

though he simply nodded, smiling. "Elizabeth."

"Azmah."

His departure sent her back the passage.

*   *   *

Azmah hurried to his next assigned job. It was risky to continue to meet Elizabeth. Mostly because he didn't understand this strange fascination between them. Also interesting, how did he know what to do when ever Elizabeth seemed about to run.

Azmah shrugged his shoulders, continuing his stride, passing several shebnis while making the turn to go to Bajith-Hethebed. Bera wouldn't be in and he would like time to prepare for their coming encounter.

A shiver rippled through his frame when thinking of the coming encounter for he dreaded when required to meet for the purpose of information. They never looked at him directly of course so he did know they were connected to the beast. Supposedly they were the first few to be attached.

Why had he been able to hide so that he was free? Each time he asked the question, he arrived at the same conclusion: he didn't know. Yet somehow he could see how he could work with those who did and not be detected. He'd grown accustomed to the side glances and when meeting them, did the same.

Over the cycles, those in charge moved him up in responsibility.

Azmah remembered vaguely when the deuel had been spoken and when it ceased. When the shebni had spoken to him, it triggered part of the old teaching.

He entered his sleeping quarters coming face to face with a shebni who looked startled, then scared, slipping out. Normally Azmah would not be here and his entrance broke apart a small circle of five from the younger house. They dispersed immediately and for a moment he watched them go sensing a slight feeling of unease. What had they been doing here anyway?

As the last shebni exited, Azmah heard the softest whisper, "Pekahiah!"

Strangely reassured he wandered over to his arpad thinking. With the exception of Ozni, he'd assumed he was the only true sight marked by clear eyes. He'd noticed Ozni's careful deliveries and learned of him and then Anna and now Elizabeth. So these could either be free or want it!

Steps outside the room spurred him up off his arpad, passing the one who entered. His appointment must not be late and he must not miss anything from this point on. Azmah hurried to his meeting missing the startled gaze of the shebni he'd left behind.

*   *   *

Azzan viewed the rapid departure of Azmah with mixed feelings. Of the five he'd been assigned the job of speaking to this older shebni and been afraid to do it. At the same time he'd wanted like the others to know if what they'd heard was true and could he be trusted. Joshua said he could and Joshua should know since he was the one who had come up with the special word.

It really was special. Azzan could feel it. Though not enough cycles to remember, he only knew it did something to his insides when spoken. It was good that he wasn't hooked up to the beast like some of the others.

At this point he caught a glimpse of someone coming and quickly left for his assigned task. He went by way of their secret path dropping down into the lower part of the house. He had to let the others know he had not talked to Azmah yet and couldn't wait for he didn't want to be caught loitering by Akkub. His traitorous eyes seemed to see everything.

*   *   *

Akkub's eyes spotted the retreating figure. Too bad, he fumed, turning to retrace his steps. He needed evidence to bring to Bera. They wanted to prove the beast's methods false. And even though they were connected yet they were noticing things the beast was missing.

To speak of these things was forbidden and done only in the utmost secrecy. Bera's instructions were most specific for if Abaddon or Ahithophel suspected they could program the insert to receive and listen in on conversations. If unapproved of the direction being talked about, it could punish. Squashing the surge of fear that thought generated, he arrived at Bera's office just in time to see another figure leaving.

*   *   *

Azmah was hurrying to his next post mind reeling under the impact of what he had just heard. He'd known they were watching but not how much. Apparently Bera knew more about him than he had realized even though the machine did not. He no longer had time to check the passage since Bera required his appearance every spare moment. As he moved he noticed new shebnis working around him and they seemed to see his every step. He had not been able to pass on his new knowledge to Joshua or any of the free sight.

However he had noticed in the meetings Bera made no mention of Joshua so maybe it wasn't too bad.

*   *   *

Joshua had several narrow escapes. If he hadn't talked with Elizabeth they would have frightened him enormously. Meanwhile they made him very careful.

The next attempt came when a younger bahurim slid past him and whispered, "Pekahiah!" He'd been schooling himself not to react since the last try so he kept working at his task. It gave him a head's up though so as he worked he glanced side ways and saw the same bahurim who had tried before. This time he was talking with an older shebni who was well known as an athurim. That one Joshua knew was very nasty.

The final try came at mid meal. Joshua had a bite in his mouth when he felt someone standing behind him He barely had time to swallow when the pain hit coming in waves. Anger and amazement swarmed him for he didn't know why but he'd had it. He needed a way from the pain.

When Joshua came to the pain still rolled though he was now able to keep awake. He'd been placed in a room with only one door and a tapestry hanging on the opposite wall. The rest was bare though extremely dirty as if unused. His awakening co-incited with the entrance of an assir who took one look and left. He heard the door lock leaving him

alone and still hurting. Why was he here? What was happening? One word formed in his mind.
He whispered, "Pekahiah."

*   *   *

Azmah was in route to his next class on how to deliver naamas. When the urge hit to deviate from his normal route, he almost resisted but made the turn. Seeing the first door he followed the urge. The lock didn't stop him and his look inside made him step inside re-locking the door.

*   *   *

Words were useless. Azmah grappled with multiple questions while releasing Joshua. Then remembering the passage room where Elizabeth had stepped behind the tapestry he tested this one. They found themselves in between two tapestries. The next room opened up to the usual route he took to his class and had actually shortened his steps. Silently he led Joshua making sure no one was around. Amazingly the halls to the passage door were also clear. They entered letting the door close, standing still until a shadowy figure rose.
"Elizabeth?"
"Azmah?"
Elizabeth had just about come to the end of her

vigil. She'd been there since the shahar meal. Sight of the two figures brought sudden fear and it had taken all her courage to stand. Realization set in as she recognized Joshua and his condition.

In the dim light his eyes were red and his face pinched almost blue in color. Her trained eyes saw the side effects of extreme pain revealing his ongoing torture.

She spared one glance for Azmah before taking Joshua's arm. He stiffened at the unfamiliar touch.

Azmah flushed then nodded at the slight smile she passed on and quickly exited. His entrance in class was remarkable for he was right on time. His opening remarks co-incited with a shebni sticking his head in the door. He had a peculiar expression on his face at seeing Azmah and immediately with drew. Recognizing his face as some one he'd seen watching Azmah breathed a sigh of relief. His disappearance gave Azmah a trace of a smile of satisfaction. Joshua was safe and he'd made it in time.

*   *   *

Wracked by pain, Joshua submitted easily to Elizabeth's instructions to lie down.

"Let the pain carry you. Don't fight it. If you pass out, It's alright. I'm right here." She wasn't sure if her instructions penetrated the torture he was feeling though he lay peacefully enough.

Something had prompted her to come equipped with asa materials and she readied the shot as his body suddenly began thrashing wildly. His eyes showed the lack of thinking while the body twisted and jerked as if to escape the pain and live. The abrupt slump brought her up on her knees. When his breathing stopped, she punctured his skin doing what she'd done to Sarid. Almost forgetting as she noticed the shot not working, a surge of memory prompted her near yell.

"Pekahiah!"

Phase 5: Haziel- Vision

Isaiah 43:19 Behold I will do a new thing. Now shall it spring forth; Shall ye not know it?

Again she heard the sound of a second husky voice blending with hers and turned around.

A figure resembling Azmah stood facing her. Yet while Azmah was smooth faced, this one was hairy. And his salmas flowed white almost lighting the room much the same as sisamai lit the over heard. His glowing brightness seemed about to overwhelm her and she unconsciously bowed her face to the dusty floor in front of her.

"Rise my daughter. Your prayer has been heard. The bahurim lives."

Movement to her right confirmed his words as Joshua weakly struggled to raise an arm reaching to the back of his head.

"My little one, I have more to bring. Be always ready. Elizabeth!" His speaking her shem brought her to her feet. "I have put you here for this purpose. There is a destruction coming but I am sending you help to lead everyone out. Remember, Pekahiah gets you help."

The figure's departing words came as his figure vanished leaving Elizabeth staring for a moment. She rejoined Joshua on the ground. His weak grin brought a slightly bemused one from Elizabeth.

"I feel different."

"You have been kicked out. You no longer exist to the beast."

"Then why do I have air going in and out."

"I restarted you. With Pekahiah. You'll have to rebuild your strength and relearn several things. One is walking upright. Come on, let's get you to my place. You are free now."

When he heard those words, a shaft of joy floated through his body supplying the strength needed to rise up. Elizabeth's touch rippled through him. Unaccustomed as he was yet he welcomed the warmth it generated. Their progress was very slow but when they arrived beneath the chemosh hiding area, Joshua felt much better. Sarid's amazed exclamation brought smiles as she greeted them.

"I see you made it. It's hard at first but it gets easier. Sit here, How did you come out?"

Elizabeth helped Joshua take his seat before answering. "He's like you only the beast found him out. He's been removed."

Joshua settled himself getting a better position. "I'm not sure I know a lot. After I talked to you last, I got more contacts. Then something went wrong. I don't know what. I'd done what you said and it had paid off. Then things went wrong and more problems appeared. I ended up like this because someone tripped the beast's control by touching the back of my neck. The next I knew someone looked in on me, I got scared, and whispered the word you told me. Azmah immediately entered, released and led me out to you." His speech tired him and he stopped.

Sarid quickly said. "Rest now, we'll talk more later."

Elizabeth motioned to Sarid and they went up to the lookout. While watching around she told what she'd seen in the vision. Sarid stared at her in amazement.

"He said he's sending someone?"

"Yes, said there would be more than you two also."

"Then it is good we are stocked full of supplies."

" I think we are going to need more." Elizabeth said and Sarid looked at her shocked.

Containers of zibas both dried and fresh filled the supply area below the chemosh. Heaped to the top it now filled the rondure enclosure, Sarid had made many containers and prepared it all. Many times Elizabeth had been thankful for her having come.

Shahar brought many more developments. Elizabeth made an early trip through the passage to make contact with Azmah filling him in on Joshua's condition. She didn't stay long.

With Joshua gone, Azmah would come across one of the bahurims who know him through Joshua. Hearing his whisper, "Pekahiah", Azmah waited for the end of class.

Giving a nod, he started walking. If the bahurim was serious he knew to follow Azmah to a room he'd chosen that didn't seem to be too used. It was at the boundary of the bahurim. He told him to wait until the zereda meal and help would come.

As each bahurim approached, he found it harder and harder to get free space in between classes. Several times his next class should have started but had to wait for his arrival. Of course his lessons were prepared by Ahithophel so they weren't hard to use. He basically said the same thing for each senuah.

When he checked back, Elizabeth hadn't returned yet. Not used to sitting still, the eight bahurims were finding it hard to stay in place. By zereda, Azmah was finished with his last class, though he knew he'd have to talk with Bera later giving a report. He joined the bahurims where they waited. They greeted him with a sigh of relief.

Elizabeth appeared just as Ozni entered the room. Azmah turned to look in amazement. But Elizabeth's arrival drew his attention. He drew near to her eagerly.

"I have eight."

"Yes, you will have even more." She filled him in on she had seen.

"Are you sure? Maybe someone slipped in."

Elizabeth drew back and shrugged. "As far as I know, what he said was the truth. He knew the helping word- Pekahiah. When I do asa and say the word, it works."

She turned to the others who were watching them and smiled. The next instant she felt a jolt in the pit of her stomach that stiffened her spine and opened her mouth.

The voice of Kolaiah echoed through the chamber. "My people, who hear my voice. I am with you. Be ready when the time comes. I have heard your cries and am sending you help. Listen well to their instructions. Jehu is my shem. The two I will be sending are known as Shamah and Raguel. The time is close when I will destroy the old and bring in the new. Watch, be ready for I will come at a time when they do not expect and will do as I have said. I am Jehu!"

The voice stopped and Elizabeth slumped. She would have fallen had not the two closest to her caught her. The rest were staring open mouthed in wonder and fear at the extreme power they'd felt while she'd spoken. In herself, Elizabeth wasn't one to draw attention.

Azmah drew closer. "So we know the vision is real. Even what the beast has been telling is partially true only not the way it tells it." He turned to Ozni.

"There are still others who need to be set tree. We must continue to give them the word, Pekahiah and if they accept it we will know they are called and hear. Even as all of us have heard."

Sounds of running feet got their attention.

Instantly all nine escaped under the tapestry. Azmah and Ozni watched Elizabeth lead the bahurims before re-entering the chamber the Adinos had vacated. Quickly they resumed their next assignments undetected.

Leading, still numb from her electrifying charge that had accompanied Kolaiah's voice, Elizabeth fought an odd weakness as she brought the bahurims to the chamber where Joshua had hid.

The weakness was odd in its effect cause in an odd way she was stronger in one sense even while feeling weak. Giving the eight instructions she watched them lie down at the first sign of pain.

"This is not going to be easy." She spoke to each one. "Let the pain take you, relaxing makes it easier and faster. I will be with you."

Some grasped the idea and submitted at once. Others didn't find it so easy and fought against it. Elizabeth quickly understood: it was one thing to endure when you had to but quite another when a simple action could take it away. They had to make up their minds and stay determined.

Coniah was the first to drop. His body jerked aggressively before growing slack. Aziza's body gave an explosive shudder snapping his neck next. Then he was still. Azmon came after him though not as violent.

Elizabeth moved among them giving the shot and speaking as she ministered asa. All three came alert immediately smiling weakly when they realized their worst fear was over. Ahasai had time to see the three smile. Seeing them gave him confidence and he surrendered. Ahumai quickly followed letting his body flop and struggle. Gibbar was quick to pass out. Isaac and Jarib were last.

When everyone reawakened and were on their feet, Elizabeth led them very slowly to the meeting room where they were welcomed by Joshua. It was then they knew they weren't dreaming and dropped to the ground. Walking had tired them. Joshua quickly assured them, the feeling would pass.

Elizabeth reminded them of the need to be quiet for she knew sounds carry. She didn't want them to be rediscovered or herself to be found. Her freedom to move around was not in jeopardy for she used it sparingly, never in the open unless during cush. But the plans would be betrayed.

Those in charge knew the ones who belonged. When the beast kicked out the inserts of those who ceased to exist, their presence should not be seen.

This presented a problem Elizabeth was unsure how to handle. The room was getting full and the more set free, the more she had to hide and feed. Sarid and her helpers were doing well with what Elizabeth had stored but the supplies were vanishing faster than she could afford to restore.

One senuah after she had raided the alamoth's guni she stared at the small amount laying at her feet and the empty space before her. In a moment of hopelessness she whispered, "Jehu, I slip out and bring what I can but it's not enough to keep up. You'll have to send help."

Two senuahs later that help arrived in an unexpected manner as two bahurims entered their guni at the first hint of sisamai's light.

Elizabeth had been woken by one of the bahurims who turned over loudly in his sleep. Finding herself unable to go back to sleep, Elizabeth rose and mounted watch. The fact the bahurims were in the guni so early made her keep a close eye on their actions. Strangely they kept their heads down as if in hiding. It made her watch for any danger.

The shorter of the two carried a chellubi into which he piled zibas as fast as they dug. The second did the same with carpus. At the same precise moment they looked around at one another, nodded and sauntered casually to their boundary. Elizabeth heard running feet and glimpsed Ahasbai running down the path towards the two who had dropped their burdens. He approached what they left leaping out in the open, lifting the chellubis, ducking back under. His heavy load made Elizabeth drop and join him grabbing one of the loads.

Sarid was waiting in the supply room. They unpacked both. First Elizabeth took time to make a tally with Sarid then let her put everything a way. It would do for a while. She dropped her head a moment. "Thanks Jehu."

Next senuah, Elizabeth entered the passage to the castle she heard a strange cry. Strange at least for that sound didn't belong since even the free young were in the houses. The cry wasn't close either. It drifted along on the breeze that blue through the rooms and Elizabeth was hard pressed to track it.

In wide eyed wonder she entered a room where lay five small naamas. The startled figure of an older alamoth rose facing her and she met the true gaze seeing free sight. In a flash she understood.

"They were in danger?"

Anna's stiff form nodded, not knowing who she was facing.

"How did you get them here?" Anna's shrug answered giving Elizabeth cause to hesitate and then she smiled. "I'm Elizabeth."

The stiffness dropped like a removal of a salma and Anna responded eagerly. "I didn't know. I'm Anna. Ahithophel ordered a check of birth records. When he sent the order I knew it wouldn't match and snatched these five. I have Habaiah. Somehow I had to get her out."

"Are there more?"

"Yes," Anna looked at her helplessly. "What do we do?"

"Can you go back?" Elizabeth was thinking

quickly.

"I think so. As long as the check is not completed."

"You must get as many as you can. Take them to the closest guni. I'll have someone waiting. I'll take these with me. Let's hurry."

Frightened Anna went. Elizabeth wrapped the five in her outer salma returning to the hiding place. Sarid was so glad to see Habaiah she didn't realize the implications. Joshua though took one look and jumped to his feet. Elizabeth came closer.

"I need you to go to the guni's edge closest to the naamas. Wait there for another delivery of free-borns. Ahithophel has commanded a bed check."

His gaze flickered and he leaped to the look out. He disappeared while she settled the little ones in make shift arpads.

Ozni was nonplussed when he entered Beth-shan. Another alamoth was doing Anna's job. Her side glances made him hesitate about staying until he caught sight of Anna's return. He arrival had been silent and with the other alamoth there no words were exchanged.

Suddenly Ozni knew what she was thinking. "Five who can walk?" Even though the other alamoth had stepped into the other room, his words were low.

"Yes, now! Out in the guni." She stepped into the other room where the little ones were sitting around on big blocks of wood and various rocks. They were put there to keep them occupied, and taught. Not knowing these as well as the naamas, she approached each one watching the eyes. Most evaded hers and she passed half the line before getting the five. In an effort not to alarm the rest, she took their hands. Surprised at the unusual touch, they nonetheless responded to it and followed.

When she passed Ozni she stopped, knelt looking directly into each set of eyes before putting their hands into his. No one made a sound. Possibly from shock or knowing, she stood as they left.

Reaching the birth records she pulled the naama five first then these alamoths. It was then that she almost got caught. The alamoth had returned from taking care of the naama Ozni had brought and now came carrying the file to where Anna worked . Anna heard the squeak of the door in time to step to an young alamoth starting to cry. It gave Anna an excuse to pick her up, She didn't see the side glance thrown as the alamoth drifted close.

She did see the eyes watching every move she now made. It prepared her for the questions which followed. They came had and fast.

"Where did you go?"

"I had an errand."

"Why are some missing?"

"Are there some missing?" Anna threw her a startled look. "What do you mean?"

The alamoth glanced in her direction. "I don't know. It's just that I thought there were more than what I see now."

The answer gave Anna relief and made her watch the alamoth closer. She laid the naama down. "Well, check the records. They should all be listed."

"Is that what you were doing?"

That question was too close to the truth, Anna shoved her hands in the salma folds to hide their trembling. What was the alamoth wanting?

"Because if you were, I want to help." The words burst out as if pent up inside."

Anna gave a brief nod. "Let's get busy." She still had to remove the last five shems. This would give her the chance.

*   *   *

Joshua reached the edge of the temple's fallen pillars. The nearest guni was still several steps away. By shielding his eyes he could see past the open area and spied the small file being led. He darted out greeted Ozni and grabbed the first alamoth's hand. Ozni faded away as Joshua herded the five into the pillars' shadow. He looked down at the small hand. She gazed up at him and their eyes met. He grinned as she stared. This looked to be the first of many.

And it was. With the ruins in the center of

both younger houses little ones were constantly being shifted. Anna never let up in her search for free sight and neither did Ozni. The ones with the chip never cried unless being corrected. So those who cried were checked well. Elizabeth wondered about those in the older houses who never came to the naama Beth-shan. They weren't in as much danger for the record search hadn't reached them yet.

On one of Ozni's frequent stops was bringing new naamas, Anna had none to send back so she sent word about her concern in the older cycles . Azmah was able to have his meeting with Elizabeth where they talked over the problem.

Elizabeth looked thoughtful. "I'll talk to Kolaiah about it."

"That's good, Elizabeth."

His use of her shem never failed to make her feel strange and he immediately noticed the slight flush staining her neck, rising up to her cheeks. The warmth in his chest was reflected in his eyes and he slid his arms tentatively around hers.

Unsure of the weird feeling racing through her, Elizabeth none the less enjoyed the warmth this kind of touch generated. In spite of the newness she didn't jerk back like before but leaned into the pleasantness. His closeness made her heart beat faster and she felt unable to move away.

"Elizabeth?" His husky voice had deepened and it made her head swim.

"Azmah what? What's going on?"

"I want this." he leaned his head forward and awkwardly placed his lips on her face to the side of her mouth. Startled at the touch she turned her head and their lips met. Heat radiated inside and their arms tightened as the kiss deepened. The currant between them gathered strength until Azmah broke the connection taking a breath while gazing down on Elizabeth's dazed eyes.

"What was that?" She managed to ask as her insides continued spinning.

Unwilling to let go, Azmah took another breath. "I'm not sure. I don't know why I even wanted to do that but I'm glad I did." Talking helped him to pull away releasing her reluctantly.

Touching her lips with her fingertips, Elizabeth smiled. "I am too. True I am wondering what happens from this. It certainly feels good."

Her words stirred him and the warmth in his eyes darkened them drawing Elizabeth but she some how refused.

"I should return." His eyes softened.

"You are right. So should I. Elizabeth."

"Azmah," Her nod sent him on his way smiling over the wonder of it all. She paused a minute hearing his footsteps diminish.

"Pekahiah, Kolaiah. What should be done about the older alamoths?"

"I have set one in place who is hiding them.

I'll bring them later."

"Thanks Kolaiah." She hurried back to the meeting room. Sarid would like to know.

Sarid was not in the meeting room which was lined with shebnis of various cycles. Clustered together Elizabeth noticed most were no longer frightened but had been put to work. Sarid met her at the food storage area entrance.

"More will be coming. Kolaiah says some one is hiding them."

Sarid nodded holding a bundle. Elizabeth realized it was Habaiah. She smiled kindly at the little one and Sarid responded.

"She knew me. I don't know how, but she knew me. Everyone else made her cry but when I took her, she got quiet." Tears threatened but Sarid overrode them. "Do you know when we leave?"

"When the promised ones come. Kolaiah said there would two, bahurim and alamoth. I know no more."

" A few bahurims have trickled in. These have free sight."

Elizabeth's brow creased. "It's a wonder the beast doesn't know where we are."

"Maybe it does."

Elizabeth shook her head slowly. "I don't think so."

*   *   *

Abaddon shook his head at Ahithophel's words and the beast's read out sheet. "You mean we have lost this many over the last fifty senuahs?"

Ahithophel in answering was shaking his head even as Abaddon spoke. "I don't understand it. But something has hit the bahurims and alamoths. They are disappearing. I've sent the adinos and they aren't even finding bodies. It is as though they vanish."

"Can you reprogram the beast?"

"I've tried but the circuits don't respond. It has bypassed my programming and refuses my instructions."

Abaddon stared rudely, black eyes glaring. "but YOU created it. Just turn it off."

Ahithophel shook his head. "Doesn't make any difference. I've tried everything. It just repeats the facts, they no longer exist. When I try to retrace the body whereabouts it blocks my efforts. Almost as if anticipating my actions."

Abaddon waved his hands. "Well you've gotten us in a fine mess. You'll just have to deal with it.. It is in your hands. Now what else do you have to talk about?"

"Some of the younger houses have been coming up short on food delivered. They claim they'd sent the amount needed but the assirs have no report of deliveries received. The beast reports the bahurim made the deliveries yet none is recorded.

"Tell them they will need to make up the difference. The run was made just not enough. Increase their work in the gunis. And if that doesn't work, we will start sending the adinos for the food." He patted his ample belly.

Ahithophel rose from the arpad. "That covers all I have except for Bera and his complaints."

Abaddon rose too staring at his heavy form, face fierce. "Just do what you can. Bera need proof and there isn't any. He's wasting his cycle."

*   *   *

Bera knew Azmah was free sighted. How he knew, he couldn't have said but Abaddon was right, he needed proof. The main problem: Azmah was good, very good at what he did. The one drawback: he had unexpected absences.

Bera preferred athurims to get his information. Even with the chips they were reliable. They had verified Azmah turning up a little later than expected or leaving a little earlier than warranted, Then there were those in the older house who were acting different. How different Bera couldn't exactly put his finger on but he knew it.

Bera, himself, had an implant and while he didn't understand how it worked, it didn't hinder him from doing anything he wanted. Like right now he was heading to the lower level to get a bite to eat even though sisamai had long ago set and all food preparation had ceased. But he had access to the extra supplies and knew how to visit them and the workers when ever he wanted. It was part of his usual routine.

His entry coincided with Azmah's return though Azmah emerged in time to close the door and step away before Bera entered the hall. Breathing calmly he halted as Bera advanced.

"Out getting yourself an extra bite?"

Bera queried as he scrutinized Azmah's face. He caught Azmah's facial twitch before glancing away. Was that relief or fear he saw?

Azmah answered, "Thought I'd look a round. Though nothing appealed to me." Only Elizabeth, Azmah thought then squashed the memory.

With his own mind on food Bera turned toward the food preparation area where extra food lay, handy.

"I'll catch you at shahar." His parting words sent Azmah to the sleeping section of Bajith-Hethebed. His steps took him past a door not normally used. Hearing scuffling noises and a soft cry, he stopped in his track. Pushing on the door released the catch and Azmah could see two shebnis fighting. One was Abaddon, the other an alamoth from the older section of Succoth-Benob. Abaddon got the upper hand and forced the alamoth down.

In a sudden rage Azmah shoved the door open,

entered and using all his strength slammed Abaddon on the back of the head. He fell releasing the alamoth. She gathered her torn salma trying to rise.

"What have you done? The beast will hurt you."

Azmah gave her a hand and recognized an alamoth who had delivered a naama not long ago. "Wasn't he hurting you?"

"Yes, but it's not the first." The look she gave was open and straight. His expression went from quizzical to anger.

"You are free. You don't need to do this."

"I do it to keep free. I just can't seem to stop fighting."

"Come. I have a place for you to hide. There's no need for you to be subject to this abuse."

His words were accompanied by his step towards the door when he heard other steps coming. Their exit behind the tapestry coincided with Bera's appearance. His eyes focused on the body lying on the floor not on the tapestry movement, When he saw Abaddon's body moving, he left. Abaddon would put the blame on him if he was present.

Delivery made, Azmah hurried to Bajith-Hethebed. He was supposed to be sleeping. A sense of warning cued him in on a possible problem. It was just a matter of time before his many escapes would cause him to get caught. But perhaps Jehu would come before then.

Phase 6: Tehaphnehese: The beginning of the End.

Ecclesiastes 3:1   To everything there is a season

Elizabeth gazed with awe at the odd assortment filling the room beneath the chemosh. Not one naama was crying. For the most part, Anna had sent all she knew, though she herself had not come yet. She'd sent word she was helping a second group hidden under ground.

Azmah had not come yet either nor Ozni. Elizabeth could sense the time approaching but wasn't sure of their reasons for staying in place. Possibly to help others yet. She knew it wouldn't be long.

The promised one from Beth-Alamoth had not yet arrived either. On this senuah Elizabeth was undecided on how to approach Jehu again. Unable to make up her mind, she slipped away to the chemosh perch. One glance put her in motion.

A small line of alamoths were coming out the side entrance of Beth-Alamoth. She counted eight as one by one they walked straight ahead. The slight figure in front was the only head looking back and forth though as early as it was, no other alamoth came near or even appeared to be watching. Maybe it was because no problem had been expected. At any rate the eight alamoths ranging from very short to Elizabeth's height headed directly to the tumbled down pile of temple ruins. The fact they never hesitated gave Elizabeth assurance the leader had heard from Kolaiah. Elizabeth dropped to the path running to find Sarid. Moments later she met the leader on the path Joshua used when he would visit. Though tiny the leader faced her staunchly.

"Pekahiah. I'm Elizabeth."

"I'm Eshton and this is Erastus." Her body stiffened then relaxed accompanied by a small smile. She pointed to the tall willowy bland next in line. "Jehu sent us. Pekahiah."

"We've been expecting you. Just follow the path." Eshton nodded, green eyes flashing brightly. She took the lead as instructed. Elizabeth smiled as each passed clearly showing their free sight. The last one gave her pause for the vision was not as clear as it should have been. She studied her closer. Hair long, not entirely clean, salma was reasonably clean yet it didn't seem right. A slightly secretive feeling seemed to come over Elizabeth.

Shaking the feeling off, she resumed her seat in the chemosh among the pillars. The passage of the alamoths had not been noticed, she was thankful to see, though by now most everyone else was out doing their work. She waited a while longer before rising and leaping down below.

"Pekahiah!" The alamoth who stood before her looked like no other Elizabeth had ever seen. Eyes and hair brightly shining she seemed wrapped in a shimmer quite like sisamai's light. Without hesitation Elizabeth bowed.

"Pekahiah! You are the expected one."

The figure reached out lifting Elizabeth's face

upward.

"Yes, I am Shamah, Do not bow to me. Bow to no one but Benaiah and Jehu. I was once like you. I am here to help prepare. The time is almost here for the final destination. Let us go and meet the others for those still in place are coming."

Elizabeth stood as Shamah seemed to almost float leading the way. When they entered the room, an unusual sight met her eyes. The alamoth she'd noticed earlier was in the center of the room. Several bahurims were within arm's length holding on to her arms. One real young one ran to meet Elizabeth.

"She's Rahab. She has free sight but it's not true. She struck Erastus."

Shock at her words spurred Elizabeth but the warm hand on her arm made her step aside. She watched Shamah come forward confronting Rahab who by now was fighting hard against those holding her. Elizabeth recognized Coniah, Aziza, and Azmon.

Shamah didn't even try to speak until she stood directly in front and pinned the alamoth with her gaze. As the heat of her glance penetrated the mind of the alamoth, her struggles diminished then vanished.

Sensing the battle over the three bahurims slowly lightened their grips then stepped aside. Rahab never saw for the heat of Shamah's gaze had cut the uncleanness of her own sight. She suddenly realized what she had been ready to do.

"I'm so sorry. I really am. Please don't make me leave. I never would have promised if I'd known."

"Who approached you?"

"I don't know. He said he was from Bera and promised me, I'd be a personal assir if I did as he asked."

"So what do you want?"

Rahab looked around. "To stay here. I don't care what he promised. It was all lies. Don't send me away."

Shamah held her gaze for an endless moment then nodded. "You are telling the truth. You are no longer Rahab, I call you Joanna by order of Benaiah. Elizabeth, she needs to wash."

She studied Joanna, "You will go with her?"
Joanna nodded, head held high. "Yes."
"Good."

*   *   *

Azmah's duties had him checking out the food prep area just as Bera wanted to find out what he'd been doing there. And as much as Azmah wanted to see Elizabeth, something told him not to bother checking on her: she wouldn't be there. On his final round he spied the room where Joshua had been hid standing ajar.

With most doors shut the open door made him stop and step inside. No one was present. He turned reaching for the door to leave.

"Azmah!" He paused looking back.

The bahurim facing him looked like no other bahurim Azmah had ever seen. The salma he wore flowed as if lit by sisamai. His face and hair shone even brighter.

Without conscious thought Azmah sunk to his knees. Immediately the figure sprang forward.

"Do not bow to anyone else except Benaiah or Jehu. I am Raguel. Kolaiah told you of my coming."

Azmah's face wore a smile so bright it almost rivaled the glow around Raguel. "I have come to tell you to pass the word along to those still in place. Pekahiah, come out and join the other free sight below the temple. I'll meet you there."

On the final words he vanished. Azmah wore a dazed look. He stepped out in the hall in time to see Bera heading towards him.

"Ahithophel needs you below. Be quick about it."

As usual Azmah turned to obey but something caught his attention and he slowed. That cunning gleam in Bera's face told him something was off. Raguel's appearance had a purpose. It had to be a warning. A trap was set.

Swinging by Bajith-Hethebed, he spied those same shebnis meeting near their arpads. Striding past he spoke.

"Pekahiah, follow me to a safe place. Now, quickly."

His actions gave no chance of alternative decisions and Azzan leaped up immediately. The entire group moved as one as Azmah took a round about course to the passage entrance. Putting a hand to the door, he shoved to show Azzan, then vanished to his assignment.

One more and he was out of here. He thought. Ozni wasn't in his usual place so reluctantly Azmah headed for Ahithophel and the beast's room.

His steps slowed upon seeing the door. He never liked to come here and always approached with caution. Now he saw Ozni vanishing around one of the corners in the hall and broke into a run to catch him. At that instant a shout came from behind.

"He's getting away.!"

The terrible sound of running feet spurred Azmah into an all out sprint. Catching Ozni, he grabbed for his hand. He caught it and discovered it weak and soft. Again he knew! But it didn't matter. Thanks to his experience with Elizabeth he wasn't leaving Ozni behind, even if he wasn't free sighted. As he gripped Ozni's hand he didn't get any resistance either and a quick look at his face let him know Ozni was resolute. At least for now.

Hearing sounds of approaching feet, Azmah ducked into a room-same one where he'd rescued the alamoth. He needed the tapestry. The next room contained two additional tapestries and passage. This passage exited near the food prep area. From there Azmah and Ozni were safely on the other side of the secret door. The ones he'd left there were still waiting. They greeted him warmly.

Loud running sounds sent Azmah into further action as he remembered what Elizabeth had discovered. This place was no longer safe.

"Pekahiah," the word burst from his lips as he pulled Ozni, he led the group in the direction she'd come. Ducking beneath the first tapestry gave a welcome reward of diminishing sound. He didn't stop though. But now Ozni was fighting.

When Ozni first felt Azmah's hand, he wasn't sure was was expected and he remembered he liked Azmah. To his surprise he found a small part of him did not want to go with him. That part increased greatly when he entered the passage. The further he went, the greater it grew and when the pain hit, it swamped any previous desire to go. He had to get free of the hand and the pain. All he could think about was the pain.

"Let me go! Please let me go. I have to go back." His whimpering cry only made Azmah speed up and when his breaking point hit he started thrashing wildly. Azmah called a halt staring at the others. He could no longer make any progress hanging onto Ozni. In addition he was the only one who had the slightest knowledge of what he was doing. He had to go for Elizabeth.

*   *   *

Shamah gazed with approval at the set-up. Suddenly a picture flashed into her mind and she stiffened. "Elizabeth!" When Elizabeth turned, Shamah added. "Take your asa and go. Azmah needs you."

Her words were scarcely out as Elizabeth cleared the area sprinting into action. The rest stared after her vanishing form.

*   *   *

Placing the five shebnis around Ozni's wildly thrashing body, Azmah started out in the general direction that he knew. To his surprise and amazement he hadn't covered any ground before he could hear heavy breathing ahead. Someone was close. In fear he hid beside the tapestry, unsure whether to run or stay. He stayed.

The tapestry was flung back and he recognized Elizabeth's presence.

"Thanks Jehu. You're here." He grabbed her hand taking over the lead. While they traveled the few steps he'd come, he filled her in.

"Then it's Ozni." Her comment popped them into the room. The others didn't notice since their approach was quieter than Ozni's thrashing. He had scared the five away from him though they managed to keep him in the room. They all knew he was losing the battle. When Elizabeth approached him, he dropped to the floor, her appearance seemed to take his fight., The others jumped.

"Ozni. Let go. Ride the pain. It's alright. I'm here to help."

Her words brought an unexplained yet instant relief as he relaxed all thought. The thrashing grew more violent and she stayed out of range. At least he wasn't trying to escape now. The moment his body went limp, she moved inserting the asa in his upper arm.

"Pekahiah," she whispered.

Nothing happened for a breath. She stayed close in case she had to do something more. Then she backed up sensing more than seeing him taking a soft breath almost as a sigh. She looked up at Azmah.

His eyes told her more than words as she then could hear the heavy advancing steps. She rose to her feet.

Azmah waved at the shebnis, who responded quickly. "You can tell we have to move. As many as needed carry Ozni but let's go."

Elizabeth heard too but her feet refused to move as she saw and pointed. Azmah turned and saw too. Raguel stood there smiling as Azmah held up his hand.

"Come all of you. Raguel has this covered."

His words hung suspended as they all followed Elizabeth.

Raguel raised off the ground hands held at his sides. As the final shebni vanished, he raised one hand focusing thought through it to the ground.

For an instant all went quiet then the ground began to heave and buckle throwing rocks and boulders in the air. The walls of the room billowed first in then out. When the pursuing Adinos led by Bera entered, the walls burst. Raguel vanished.

The collapse buried the intruders. All but one. Being last in line, he was able to avoid most of the falling debris. Since the only way back was the way he'd come, a subdued Akkub returned to report to Ahithophel and Baashah.

*   *   *

A joyful reception met Elizabeth on her return. In the noise Raguel joined the party. Shamah flashed a thought to him and he smiled in answer and addressed the room.

"Very shortly, Jehu is going to unloose the deep. It has already started and we will be needed outside the walls to receive more shebnis. This area is some what protected so when they come out, bring them here."

His talk was interrupted by a rumble that reverberated in the walls of their hiding place. "Go now, shebnis. The little one's stay."

Anna entered, Raguel smiled, "Good, you made it. Stay with the little ones. They know you."

Her nod released him. "All the rest, go out through the pillars and the gates. Outside, hurry before they close the doors." He glanced at Shamah who nodded, "We will make a way to return." Ready to add more he stopped when Shamah vanished.

Though scared the shebnis were also excited. As Raguel vanished they followed instruction hiding near the walls. Elizabeth and Azmah took positions close to each other where they could see most of the other fanning out then dropping out of sight.

The rumbling from the passage was increasing when a huge force shook the stone walls. The gates were slammed shut.

Elizabeth and Azmah hid at the sight of figures on top of the wall. Each were in position near one of the rock shafts. Suddenly for no reason she could think of, Elizabeth stepped away from hers. The instant she did, one of the figures on top jumped inside. He must have panicked cause he never waited to get completely seated but pushed the release button.

Shaft and body disintegrated blowing large shards of rock in the air. The place where she'd been standing received most debris.

Glancing over at Azmah who was looking at the figure climbing above him and his closest shaft, she noticed he appeared to be doing every thing correctly but right before he shoved on the button, Elizabeth saw a piece of debris fall into his shaft. Her cry went unheard as the button was pushed.

Azmah heard the rush of air. For a split gasp of air nothing happened. Elizabeth thought it might be alright. No! The shaft exploded about halfway down. Elizabeth's shoulders drooped as she heard him scream and he ceased.

Azmah's face echoed her own as they both moved on to the next shaft in line. A figure worked at the top. Not getting in but putting someone much smaller in. For just a second she wondered then Elizabeth understood.

The shorter alamoth climbed inside as the first shebni had and second bahurim. She heard the blast of air and the bottom opened. A safe escape except for the one who was at the top. She went with the blast of air.

A little alamoth climbed out then stood as if waiting. Elizabeth let her eyes drift around the walls. She saw both Shamah and Raguel waving while hovering against a section of wall. Quickly she approached the small alamoth, took her hand leading her to their position. In amazement she stared at the large hole in the wall. Inside she could see the temple ruins.

The moment Elizabeth stepped to the hole, Eshton rose from the fallen rubble. By now the alamoth was beginning to struggle and fight as the beast applied its punishment. She wasn't where she was supposed to be so she had to be punished.

She had not fought when Elizabeth first took hold. But now she fought Eshton fiercely. As Elizabeth watched her go, she realized many more young cycles who would all need help in breaking through.

When Erastus came close, Elizabeth had her stand at the hole while she-Elizabeth went down to do what she knew best. The first was thrashing wildly against the hands which held her. It didn't last long. Again Elizabeth knew the exact moment the chip released for the body slumped. One of the alamoth's handed her asa to to her to inject. As Elizabeth did, she also whispered "Pekahiah!"

Their combined word brought instantaneous reaction. The small alamoth opened her eyes immediately. Elizabeth turned to see who helped her. Joanna! She grinned and nodded.

Things became a blur from then on for one after another the shebnis came. As they became free sighted, they quickly moved to help where ever needed.

Once Elizabeth was aware of Azmah handing her a drink. He and Sarid helped hold the thrashing bodies and wipe their faces with a slightly wet salma. A brightness let her know Shamah hovered near. Her presence gave Elizabeth more courage.

The rumble steadily increased. Even knowing they were relatively safe, the continual noise increased the pressure. Soon everyone huddled together as they drew courage from each other.

Occasionally dust billowed from the passage as other rooms crumbled while rocks shoved up through the floor.

It was a long senuah. At last the shebnis stopped coming and Shamah cautioned everyone to go to door openings where there was greater support.

They went huddled in groups, and waited. Loud thunderous claps sounded. Once more, then again. Their surroundings shook but held. No one moved. Not even the tiniest naama. Raguel appeared in the center of the room. He waved for all to come near.

They moved quickly as one. He floated to the outer edge of the huddle and began circling. Shamah did the same on the opposite side. Suddenly she stopped. Pulling up of the older alamoths she listened.

"I'm sorry, you can't be here." A wave of her

hand and she vanished along with those she pulled out. Only she reappeared. Her circle continued for a short time. Her stop put her next to a bahurim. They vanished without a word.

Raguel continued to move. He knew what Shamah was doing and why. She was removing unkind thoughts and feelings. Negative thoughts put off negative energy. It hindered the work of good since they didn't want to do good. Her work made his much easier for he was setting up a barrier against the destruction Jehu was sending. Benaiah had given both of them specific instructions. These had to be carried out to save all present.

Shamah reappeared where she'd left, making some of them jump. On her next stop, she pulled out two of the younger bahurims and six of the older. This time she didn't bother to disappear but simply sent them away.

Fearful everyone watched crowding close, doing their best not to come close to Shamah lest she take them out. Raguel stopped. His circle was complete. Shamah nodded and halted too. The air was clear. She and Raguel shared a thought.

"This is it! Let's time ourselves. Ready? One, two, three! Pekahiah Benaiah!"

With their minds clear, the entire group spoke involuntarily. To their surprise the ceiling and walls vanished. Elizabeth discovered Azmah standing near and grasped his hand firmly. She got a dim vision that the walls of the city of Ai had fallen. Indeed every building had collapsed as well. The ground where they stood rose straight up coming even with all surrounding ground. To her right Elizabeth heard yelling and looking saw a hole. She reached down along with Azmah shoving a huge rock out of the way. More shebnis climbed up out of the ground shining almost bright as sisamai. The hole closed as the last one stood on top of the ground.

They hadn't heard the temple ruins fall. Yet when she looked, they were gone. Ahead of them she could see a shining glorious building coming down and landing on the ground where the castle had stood. It was unclear exactly how huge the building was, it shone so brilliant. It lit up the entire area of the former city.

Shamah and Raguel touched down and began walking taking obvious delight in approaching the shining building. They drew others who also began to follow. Elizabeth glanced way over the open land and gasped.

In front of her very eyes the land was changing,. Hard unyielding rock dissolving into gray then brown then black dirt that darkened and became green fuzz.

Elizabeth suddenly realized Azmah was still waiting patiently and lifted her eyes to his. "It's beautiful!"

Her words were cut off as strange creatures appeared in the distance. Shouts of delight from others standing near brought her back around. They came in different shapes, sizes, and colors. Some were leaping and prancing, some came slow other ran fast. Some had horns on their heads and humps on their backs. Still they came.

"Amazing!" Elizabeth felt no fear but the urge to follow Shamah and Raguel into the huge building. It called and she answered.

Once inside, her eyes were overwhelmed by the huge amount of shebnis standing facing inward. To her surprise they parted letting those from outside enter creating a huge long passageway toward the center of what she could see now was truly a remarkable city. Only it didn't fit with what she had known. All these shebnis both alamoths and bahurims were smiling and waving. She passed some shebnis that shone so bright, she recognized them as the ones who had come out of the ground. Her eyes were having difficulty seeing.

A strange feeling come over her and Elizabeth found her face beginning to crease. Glancing at Azmah she saw his doing the same. For the first time she noticed his hair was brown and about shoulder length. He strode easily, shoulder even with her head, eyes sparkling as if reflecting the light. She didn't realize hers were doing the same.

The light! It was growing, getting brighter,

crisper. She had thought she could see before but this was different; much clearer and sharper.

They came in behind Shamah and Raguel who were approaching the strongest point of light. Sisamai was never this bright. Almost too bright to focus on, it moved up as if rising and then they saw: a tall white robed shebni who glistened all over as if he contained the light. His eyes touched Elizabeth for a moment and she experienced extreme joy in that flash. Then he addressed Raguel and Shamah.

"Well done, Raguel and Shamah. I am very proud to know you as my friends. Jehu is very happy with your obedience and will reward you richly. Here sit up on the throne for you will help judge."

They moved readily to obey releasing him. He faced Elizabeth.

"My daughter, I saw by your face, you know me. You have heard and obeyed without rebellion, no matter how hard the work was. Because of you many have been saved. I see also that you noticed something on your way in."

His warmth seemed to come over Elizabeth freeing her words. She nodded. "The land is changing, it was dead but new life has come."

His kind eyes didn't seem to leave her yet somehow he pulled Azmah into the conversation. Azmah felt suddenly alive like never before.

"Welcome, you are Azmah, truly a helper of

Jehu. You desire to be with Elizabeth and so it shall be for she wants it too."

Reaching forward he touched their hands. "I make you as one in serving me but you do not stay here. I have made a whole new world outside . This is the land of the Amad. Go out and choose a place to live together. I only require that you come to see me once every seven senuahs. Azmah, you and Elizabeth will be the first to reproduce and have a family. Do not criticize or seek to hurt each other or you will lose what you have. Go forth!"

His parting words sending them out parted those standing behind. The further they went, the better they could hear and realized he was putting other couples together.

Ozni and Anna who were given the naamas who knew no other; Azzan and Erastus, Azzah and Sarid and Habaiah, Coniah and Eshton. As the couples filed out those from the guni cheered then burst into some sort of song. One that everyone seemed to know: "Hosanna, hosanna!"

This marks the end of the Return to Ai and the beginning of forever!

Glossary

Abaddon: destroyer
Abarim: in regions beyond
Abib: green fruits or ears of corn
Abel-Meholah: meadow of dancing
Abel-Maim: valley of waters
Achbor: mouse
Adamis: men
Addi: my witness
Adino: castle guard (one who likes the spear)
Admatha: cloud of death
Agag: fire
Ahasbai: I flee to the Lord
Ahi: brother
Ahinoam: brother of grace
Ahithophel: brother of folly
Ahitub: brother of goodness
Aholiab: tent
Ahumai: brother of waters
Ai: ruins
Ajalon: stag
Akkub: insidious
Alamoths: girls
Almon: hidden passages
Amad: eternal people
Amittai: true answer
Ammah: beginning
Ammiel: one of the people of God

Amnon: a nourisher or tutor
Amraphel: one that speaks of hidden things
Anani: cloud of the Lord
Anath: answer
Anah: one who answers
Anem: two fountains
Anna: gracious
Aphek: rapid torrent
Aquila: eagle
Arahs: wanderers
Archippus: master of the horse
Ard: humpbacked
Ard Behemoth: humpbacked, colossal beast
Aridatha-Ishi: great birth-salvation
Arieh: lion
Areli: valiant, heroic
Areopagus: rocky hill
Armoni: belonging to the palace or castle servants
Arpads: beds or resting places
Arruboths: shutters
Arza: earth
Asas: doctors
Assir: servant
Athurims: spy, tale bearers
Aziel: comforted of God
Aziza: strength
Azmah: strong
Azrikam: help against an enemy
Azubah: deserted

Azzan: very strong
Baashah: evil
Bahurims: boys
Bajith-Bahurims: house of boys
Bajith-Hethebed: men's house) for older boys and men
Bakbuk: a flask
Bashan: soft sandy soil
Bavai Ebed: servant of mercy of the Lord
Bazluth-Aroer: bathhouse
Bealoth Matri: one in charge of younger (girls)
Bedan: fat or grease
Beecher: young camel
Beer-Lahoi-Roi: well of the living one who sees me
Benomi: son of my sorrow
Bera: son of evil
Betah: trust
Beth-Alamoth: house of girls
Beth-Arbel: house of God's ambush
Beth-Pelet: house of deliverance
Beth-shan: house of sleep or restructured
Bithiah: daughter of the Lord
Bithron: ravine or gorge
Boa-Nerges: sons of thunder
Bozez: bog
cabbon: cake fried in Bedan oil
Camon: his resurrection
Caphtor: container for liquid
Carpus: fruit
Charashim: crafts

Charger: platter or tray
Chellubis: backpacks
Chemarim: temple worker
Chemosh: temple fire
Cherethims: who cuts, who tears away and exterminates
Chidons: swords
Chios: snow
Chushan-rishathaim: extra wicked
Coffer: strong box
Colosse: punishment
Coniah: the strength of the Lord
Corbin: gift of God
Cush: black or nighttime
Cycles: years
Deborah: bumblebee
Demogogue: one who rules by emotional manipulations
Deuel: invocation of God
Dilean: cucumber
Dikla: a palm tree
Dishan: antelope
Dodai: beloved of the Lord
Dorcus: gazelle
Ebal: bare, stony
Eber: the region beyond
Eli: a foster son
Eliam-Legion: the god of the people with many spirits
Elim: large trees
Elizabeth: God is the oath of her
Elon: oak

En-Gannim: fountain of gardens
Eph-pha-tha: be opened
Ephron: great and choice fawn
Erastus: lovely
Eshcols: grapes
Eshton: womanly
Etam: a ravenous bird
Etham: sea bound
Ethainim: rainy season
Euroclydon: tempestuous East wind
Gammadims: spear fightings
Gehazi: valley of vision or sight
Gera bread: bread made from grain
Geshur: bridge
Gibbar: hero
Gilboa: bubbling fountain of water
Ginnethom: gardening
Habaiah: hidden of the Lord
Hakkatan: the smallest
Hon-Hegidgad: Hill of thunder
Hazormaveth: village of death
Hezion: mirror
Ibleam: devouring the people
Iconoclast: a breaker of images
Isaac: laughter
Izhad: shining
Jaare-Oregim: tapestry of the weavers
Jamin: right hand
Janum: boys sleeping quarters

Jarib: he will plead the cause
Jearim: forest of large trees (elim)
Jehu: the Lord is he
Jeriel: founded by the Lord God
Jeshanah: ancient
Joanna: the Lord is gracious
Joshua: The Lord will save
Kab: pail or bucket
Kadmiel: walking before the Lord God
Kedesh: sacred place
Kolaiah: the voice of the Lord
Korah: ice, hail
Luhith: table
Luz: an almond tree
Maaleh Accrabbim: going up of scorpions
Machpeleh: double cave
Massah: testing
Matred Ahira: one in charge of young boys' house
Mearah: cave
Meribah: strife
Mezahab: waters of gold
Migdol: castle
Mitres: headwraps
Moladah: birthplace
Naama: baby
Naphish: boys' eating area
Nergal: a light rolling or flashing with noise
Neri: light of the Lord
Nibhaz: Lord of darkness

nimrim: wholesome waters
Nisdoch: eagle
Nobah Caleb: barking dog
Obil: overseer of camels
Ornan: large pine
Othniel: lion of God
Ozni: hearing
Paran: lush vegetation
Parosh: fleas
Pathros: south land
Pekahiah: deliverance
Petra: rock
Phoebe: pure, brightened
Pi-Hahiroth: mouth of caverns
Pottage: soup
Pul: elephant
Raguel: Friend of God
Rahab: insolence
Rehel: ewe
Rei: friend of God
Rezeph: baking stone
Rhegium: earthquake
Rimmons: pomegranates
Rithmah: broom
Rohgah: copious rain
Rondure: circle
Rosh: chief
Sabtah: breaking through
Sarid: survivor, escaped

Saph: sink-place to wash
Senuah: day
Shahar: morning
Shaharaim: two dawns
Shamah: hearing
Shan: chemarim sleeping quarters
Sheba: man
Shebna: youth
Shedeur: casting forth of fire/lightening
Shem: name
Sheresh: roots
Shethar-Boznai: star bright
Shethars: stars
Shihor-Libnath: river of glass
Shimrath: divine guardian
Shual: fox
Sibbechai: thicket of the Lord
Sidon: fishing
Sisamai: sun
Sorek: choice vine
Stachys: ear of corn
Suah: sweeping
Succoth-Benoth: house for girls past age 12
Tapuahs: apples
Tarsis: doves
Tartak: moon
Tebaliah: baptized of the Lord
Tehaphnehese: the beginning of the age; earth, world
Tehinnah: prayer

Telaim: young lambs
Teman: southern quarters
The One: supreme Being-God
Tob Eliam: a city curse
Ulai: muddy waters
Uphaz: island of gold
Ur: light brought forth by sisamai
Uriel: light of God
Zelzah: noon
Zephen: north wind
Zereda: night
Zoheleth: serpent

www.ingramcontent.com/pod-product-compliance
Lightning Source LLC
Chambersburg PA
CBHW061434160726
47995CB00003B/882